IN MYSELF I BELIEVE

By Marilyn Frias

Illustrated by Hamadou Bocoum
& Caelina Eldred-Thielen
(Cee & Dou)

This Book Belongs to:

....

....

ISBN: 9781635353693

Dedication

To Chuck, Kara and Rick,

who every day by example,

inspire me to be the best version of myself.

The story of me: Who do I want to be?
Sometimes fierce, bold and free,
Sometimes scared, unsure — that's me.
It's my story and no one else's to write.

I get to decide and it takes lots of might!

I'll fill in the blanks of "The Story of Me."

It gets me so excited; it's my privilege, you see.

Only I decide who I want to be.

I will celebrate my differentness.

There is only one me!

As my imagination takes flight,

it leaves my body behind.
Lost in wishes and dreams, deep in my own mind,

I think to myself, "Who do I want to be?"
And that's when I know
There is so much more to me.

The sounds of the universe
Tell me I should wear a skirt.
Be quiet, not too loud,
Blend in with the crowd.
Be pretty and kind, and not too tough.
Be careful not to make a fuss.

I must find the magic inside of me.
I have a feeling that's the key.
My uniqueness can be geekiness
Or just showing off my sweetness.
I'll make my ***own*** choices;
They'll come from my own voices.

So I set off on my journey to find uniquely me.
Just the thought of it sets me free!
I could be wildly unpredictable
Or kinda quirky. Guess I'll see.

I tried on different faces of other peoples' lives.

But what I soon discovered

Is that only when I'm me I thrive.

Like the girl who climbed mountains far away from her home,

She was adventurous and determined, around the world she roamed.

But something deep inside said, "This is her...not me."

So here I go off again on my own journey.

I met a girl who was very brave
And sang upon a stage.
I tried to be courageous like her,
But my body shook and
My knees just caved.
And something deep inside said,
"This is her...not me."

So here I go off again on my own journey.

Next came a fighter pilot who soared the skies like a bird.
But when I tried to be like her, my tummy started to hurt.
And something deep inside said, "This is her...not me."
So here I go off again on my own journey.

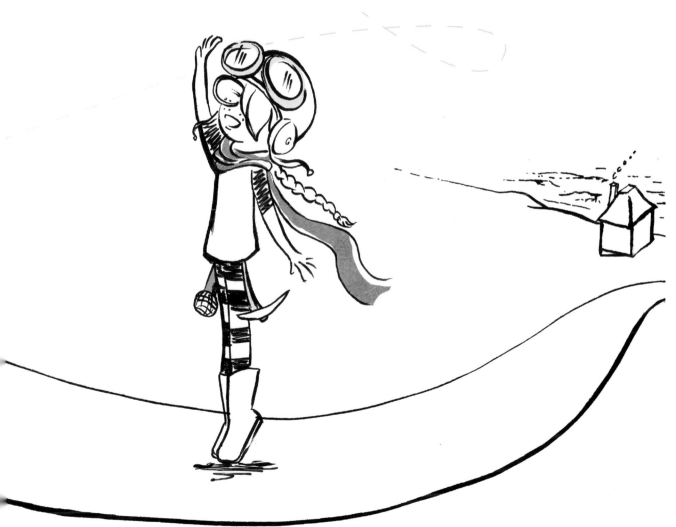

I met a poet who lived in a cottage by the sea.
Her words made me think, "Could this be the life for me?"
Her work seemed like fun, her goals lofty and large,
But when I tried to be like her, it was just too darn hard.
And a feeling deep inside said, "This is her...not me."
So here I go off again on my own journey.

Israel was my next stop, where a doctor was studying cancer.
"I'll save the world," she said to me. "I know I can find the answers."
I stayed awhile and watched her work; it was all so curious and fun.
But again I knew that this was her...not me when the day was done.

So I headed back to a place
Where it was quiet and I could think.
I began to write my own story,
Not copy someone else's,
'Cause I'm unique.

It was all just so confusing, so many voices in my head.
But what I now know is that I'm not done exploring yet!
The stuff I've learned already has made me so aware
My journey's just beginning, and I have so much to share.

I'm the boss of me and not just what everyone tells me to be.
I'll strut my stuff. Don't dare tell me that I'm not enough.
I'll surround myself with community
And those who support and believe in me.
I'll be perfectly imperfect of my own design.
There is no limit. Just watch me fly!

I will not change who is me;
It never works out well.
'Cause when you're truly not yourself,
in your heart you know.
I will hear my own rhythm.
Write my own rhyme.
Dance to a beat
That is totally mine!
I'll write the end to my own fairy tale.
Just watch me, world...I'm gonna sail!

CPSIA information can be obtained at www.ICGtesting.com
Printed in the USA
LVIW01n2309220617
539108LV00007B/63